PIP THE PIGEON : SEC

Made and printed in Great Britain by
Macs Printing, Chameleon House,
West Street, Ilminster.

Set in Calibri

ISBN Number 978-1-78926-852-2

Publisher: Independent Publishing Network
Publication date 2018

Please direct all enquiries to the author at
ptppyare@gmail.com

Acknowledgements

To write this story, I researched and did the best I could, but I admit I've made stuff up too. Well, it's a story and where would we be without imagination?

However, I wouldn't have been able to write it all without the help of many good people. These include Colin Hill, Curator at Bletchely Park. What he doesn't know about pigeons really isn't worth knowing. Jas McCorry and Elaine Zandi for their valuable input on plot and characterisation. Audrey Chiang for a great cover design, and all my family who constantly encourage, support and generally keep me going.

Thank you.

Chapter 1
A Secret is Discovered

"When's dad coming home?"

It was the summer of 1915 and Britain and Germany had been at war for a year. When it started in August 1914, men from all walks of life and from all around the country rushed to join the army or the navy, leaving their families to carry on at home without them.

Mrs Greely looked up from the pastry she was kneading and saw her son Freddie slouching in the kitchen doorway. His hands were shoved deep in the pockets of his school shorts and he was kicking at the skirting board with his left foot. She wiped her hands on her apron and walked over to Freddie. But as she wrapped her arms around him, he pulled away.

"Oh come on Freddie, love. Let me hug you."

"I don't want a hug. I want dad to come back."

"Well 'e can't can 'e? The army's got 'im now."

Freddie glared at Grumpy Bumpy, his rather bad tempered granddad who had a knobbly head and black hairy eyebrows that looked like caterpillars creeping across his forehead. Grumpy Bumpy nonchalantly continued reading his newspaper and Freddie kicked the skirting board even harder.

"Your granddad's right love. Dad's across the sea fighting the Germans." And Mrs Greely sighed and went back to kneading her pastry. "Look, I'm making your favourite, jam tarts. I made the jam this morning with all the strawberries you picked yesterday."

Freddie looked up with a spark of interest, but then let his head drop again, "But it's not the same without dad, he loves jam tarts too."

Suddenly there was a loud rustling of the newspaper as Grumpy Bumpy shook it. "Hey, listen to this. The army aren't satisfied with sending men off to war, they want pigeons now!"

Mrs Greely looked at Grumpy Bumpy, "What on earth are they going to do with pigeons?"
"Beats me, says here they're needed for important war work."

"Are you going to send yours Bumpy?" Freddie asked.

"Not likely, my loft is full of award winning birds. I don't want them flying when there's bullets..."

but before he could finish, Mrs Greely started coughing and through her wheezing asked him to get her a glass of water. As Grumpy Bumpy handed it to her, she whispered, "Don't talk about bullets, you'll give Freddie nightmares." Grumpy Bumpy harrumphed and went back to his newspaper while Freddie wandered out to the garden and the pigeon loft.

****

It was very warm and stuffy in the pigeon loft. Freddie looked at all the pigeons sitting in their coops. Some were sleeping but others were awake and ruffling their feathers or puffing up their chests. There was a soft, pleasing cooing which always reminded Freddie of water bubbling over stones. He opened a couple of windows to let some air in when the door to the loft opened.

"Ah, so you're 'ere hey?"

It was Grumpy Bumpy and he was dragging in a big sack of seed. "I don't know if I'll be able to get much more of this quality seed, the price was almost a king's ransom." He pulled the sack right into the loft, and then took the little metal cup that was hanging on a nail on the wall and gave it to Freddie.

"Here you go, give a little seed from that open sack to all the birds, there's a good lad."

Freddie took the cup and filled it with seed, then carefully went from coop to coop, pouring a little seed into each bird's dish. "Are you sure you won't send your birds to the army Bumpy? Maybe you should."

"You think so eh?"

"Well if it said important work, then yes. I mean dad went didn't he? And he didn't even wait to be asked. He signed up straightaway."

"Yep, he did that well enough."

"Well maybe if you let the army have your pigeons, they'll help bring dad home sooner," and Freddie looked at his granddad with hope in his eyes. Grumpy Bumpy looked at Freddie long and hard, then he picked up the water scoop that was on a shelf and started giving each pigeon a drink. When he finished, he turned and left the loft without another word. Left alone, Freddie went along all the birds, calling each one by name and saying goodnight. When he got to the middle coop he said, "Goodnight Pip" and moved on to the next coop when he heard, "And goodnight to you too Freddie."

Freddie spun around looking to see who had come into the loft, because he hadn't heard the door open. But there was no-one there. He stared into each corner of the loft, looking in the shadows to see if anyone was hiding there. "Come out," he shouted. "Come out and show yourself." But there was no response. He called again, but again there was no answer. Puzzled, and a little shaken, Freddie went back to the middle coop and looked hard at Pip the Pigeon. "Goodnight Pip," he said again. "Goodnight Freddie," said Pip.

Freddie leapt back in shock, then he leaned forward and looked really closely at Pip, Grumpy Bumpy's fastest racing pigeon. Known as a blue, Pip's clear red eyes shone with a bright intelligence and the feathers on his neck and breast were a shimmering green and purple in the soft evening sun that filtered through the window. The wing feathers were a light grey, mottled with a little bit of white while his leg feathers were pure white which contrasted in a delightful way with his bright orange feet. Altogether, he was a very handsome pigeon.

"You can talk! You spoke to me."

"Yes, I did and I'm sorry if I frightened you."

Freddie straightened up to his full height and said in a gruff kind of way, "You didn't frighten me, I was just taken by surprise."

Although Freddie couldn't see it, Pip smiled to himself, then said, "Of course, it is surprising for a pigeon to talk."

"It is, it is," said Freddie. Then a thought occurred to him. "Do you speak to Grumpy Bumpy?"

"Of course not," said Pip, "he'd never believe it happened. No, I shall only talk to you."

"Why?" asked Freddie, suddenly suspicious.

"Well you seem a sensible boy, and I suspect I can have sensible conversations with you."

Freddie was pleased with this answer and he smiled. Then he said, “OK, but let’s keep it as our little secret.”

“Agreed,” said Pip and then he cocked his head on one side and said, “I think your mother is calling Freddie.”

Freddie went to the loft door and opened it. His mother was standing at the top of the garden path, calling to him. “Come on Freddie, tea is ready, come in and wash your hands.”

Freddie turned back to Pip and whispered goodnight again, and left. But that night, as he lay in bed with a warm breeze blowing gently through his open window, shivers of delight and excitement ran through his body. He felt like he was on the brink of something wonderful as he thought of his new friend, Pip the Pigeon, and their fantastic secret.

Chapter 2
Lessons in Logic

"Freddie! Freddie! Where are you?" Mrs Greely had looked in his bedroom and the front room, and was now shouting from the kitchen door, in case he was in the privy in the garden. But Freddie was with Pip the Pigeon in the loft.

"I don't want to go to school, I want to stay here with you," said Freddie.

Pip turned his bright red, beady eye on Freddie. He lifted one leg from his perch, shook it and then put it back. He ruffled his wings, cleared his throat and said, "Well from what I've seen of schools, they're a good place to go."

"You haven't been," Freddie said glumly.

"But I've seen all the children running around, having fun and playing together," Pip replied.

"Well yes, playtime is good, but then we have lessons and they can be very dull."

"Ah, but at least you're learning things. And if you know things, you can make better decisions," Pip said.

"That sounds very clever, but how do you know?" Freddie asked.

But before Pip could explain more, the loft door opened and Mrs Greely stood there with her arms folded. "There you are Freddie, hurry and have your breakfast or you'll be late for school."

When the school bell rang at half past three, Freddie shot out of his desk and ran to the gate. As he was running down the street, he could hear his best friend Matthew calling after him.

"Freddie... Freddie... wait for me."

As Matthew caught up, huffing and puffing, he pulled at Freddie's sleeve to hold him back. Through his puffing, he managed to gasp out, "What's the hurry, is there an air raid? I didn't hear any sirens."

"No, there's no air raid. I just need to get home, that's all," Freddie said as he tried to pull free of Matthew's grasp. But Matthew held on tightly. "So what's so important that you're not coming to play? The gang's going to play cricket in the park. C'mon, you're our best bowler."

Freddie at last managed to pull away and as he rushed off he called over his shoulder, "Sorry Matty but I've gotta go. I'll see you on Monday." Matty stared at his friend's back as he dashed down the road and thought how odd it was for Freddie to not come and play. Then he shrugged his shoulders, turned on his heel and ran off himself, heading for the park.

****

Freddie slammed the front door, slung his satchel on the kitchen table as he passed through and ran to the pigeon loft in the garden.

"Oh, you're 'ome are you?" Grumpy Bumpy was cleaning the loft, sweeping up spilt seed and putting it back in the sack stacked in the corner. Handing Freddie the broom he said, 'Make yourself useful lad, sweep up the grain and put it in that sack." Then he rummaged in the pocket of his waistcoat for his pipe and tobacco pouch and went out into the sunny garden to have a rest.

Freddie didn't mind doing the sweeping at all. And as he worked he talked quietly to Pip. As if several hours hadn't passed since their last conversation, Freddie said, "So, how do you know that learning things helps you make better decisions?"

Pip, who had been having a little doze as it was very warm in the loft, opened his eyes and looked straight at Freddie as he said. "Well, I'm glad you listen to me." Then he shook his feathers, turned his head from side to side, looked up and down as if checking that everything in the loft was in its usual place and carried on. "You see, it's like this. When I'm out flying, I look at all the countryside that's around me. I notice buildings like churches, schools and factories. I see the roads, fields, trees and hedges. And I keep all this in mind."

Freddie expected Pip to say more, but he didn't, he seemed quite satisfied with what he'd said.

"Is that it?" he asked. "You look at things. What's that got to do with me learning lessons at school?"

Pip, who'd let his head fall forward onto his chest, lifted it with a sudden jerk and then stretched his neck. "It's just common sense isn't it?" he said, "I see all these buildings, roads and so on laid out below me and I learn them. That way, wherever I am, I always know how to get home again."

"But that's not like lessons at school," Freddie persisted.

"Maybe not," Pip replied, "but if you learn your arithmetic you can add up and subtract. That means you'll know if you get the right change when you're shopping."

Freddie nodded his head. That certainly made sense but that was only one lesson. So he leant on the broom and looked at Pip as he said, "Alright, but what about reading, why should I learn letters?"

Pip cocked his head on one side and looked Freddie in the eye. "Simple, if you can read, the whole world opens up to you. You can read adventure stories, comics, even the name of sweeties in the shops so you can choose the ones you want."

This also made sense to Freddie – he loved his comics like Victor and The

Boy's Own Paper, they were filled with adventure and exciting things like how to catch tadpoles and watch them grow into frogs. But then inspiration flashed through his mind. "What about history, why should I learn that?"

Pip, who was beginning to doze off again, opened his eyes, shook his wings and smoothly said, "History is the most important thing to learn. If you know what went before and the mistakes people made, you can try not to repeat them."

"Freddie, 'ave you swept up all them seeds yet?" And Grumpy Bumpy peered round the loft door to see how Freddie was getting on.

"Almost done Bumpy," Freddie smiled at him.

"Good, your mum says it's tea time," and Grumpy Bumpy let the door close softly as he shuffled off down the garden path.

Chapter 3
A Secret is Shared

Throughout the warm, sunny days of June and July, Pip and Freddie became firm friends. Of course, Freddie still went school but he usually dashed straight home afterwards instead of playing with his friends. Then came the school holidays and Freddie was delighted, he could spend more time with Pip. But Freddie's friend Matty wasn't going to let Freddie just disappear from the gang, so every day he called at Mrs Greely's house, asking if Freddie could come out to play. After several days of this, with Freddie constantly refusing to go out, Mrs Greely led Matty to the pigeon loft to talk to Freddie.

"Perhaps you can persuade him," she said taking Matty into the garden, "He's in there."

Matty walked up to the pigeon loft door, but just as he stretched his fingers for the handle, he heard Freddie talking. So Matty listened. He was even more surprised, because he heard two voices. One was definitely Freddie's, but the other one was softer and had a slight burble in it. Slowly, Matty pulled back the loft door and he peered in. Expecting to see Freddie and someone else, maybe a girl as the voice was so unlike a boy's, Matty was taken aback to see only Freddie and the pigeons. He waited, staring hard to see if someone was in the shadows at the back of the loft, but Freddie, feeling the presence of someone behind him, spun around.

"Matty! What are you doing here?"

"Your mum said I should come. You haven't come out to play for ages."

"Well I'm busy," said Freddie.

"Who were you talking to?" Matty asked.

Freddie felt a hot blush flush over his face, "No-one," he said and he made a move to push Matty back out through the loft door. But Matty pushed back, still searching the loft to see who else was there.

"Have you got a new friend? Is that why you won't play with us any more?"

"No," said Freddie and again he tried to push Matty out.

"I heard you," said Matty, bracing himself against the loft doorframe, equally determined not to be pushed out. "It sounded like a girl, have you got a sweetheart?" he grinned at Freddie.

Freddie blushed again, but before he could think of anything suitable to say, Pip ruffled his feathers, raised his head and said with as much indignation as he could muster, "A girl. Well, I've heard it all."

This stopped Freddie and Matty in their tracks. Matty stared at Freddie and said, "Did you hear that? That pigeon over there spoke."

Freddie was just about to deny hearing anything, because he didn't want to share his secret with Matty or anyone. But again Pip spoke up. Shaking his wings and raising his head, he said, "Yes, I do speak."

"Shhh," said Freddie glaring at Pip, but Pip just winked at him. Matty could hardly contain himself as he squirmed and pushed to see around Freddie who was trying to block him out of the loft. Matty gave a great big push and both he and Freddie fell through the door onto the loft floor. Picking themselves up, they moved together towards Pip. Freddie's instinct was to stand in front of Pip and shield him from Matty, but Matty was quicker and got to Pip's coop first. Staring hard at the pigeon, he asked, "Have you always been able to speak?"

Pip thought this was funny and gave a short, burbling laugh. "Did you speak as a baby?" he replied.

Matty thought about this, and then said, "Hmm, clever answer."

Freddie had had enough of this, and he pulled Matty back. "Look," he said, "you've got to keep this secret. No-one else knows that Pip can speak."

Matty looked at his friend, and then at Pip. "OK," he said, "I'll keep it secret, but you've got to let me come and play with you and Pip."

"That's a wonderful idea," Pip cooed before Freddie could say a word.

Freddie looked from one friend to the other and then smiled. "Yes, we'll be our own new gang!"

Just then the loft door flew open and Grumpy Bumpy came in. "Oh, you're all in 'ere are you? Well you can make yourselves useful, and 'elp me tidy up."

As the boys helped Grumpy Bumpy sweep, fill the water dishes and stack the seed sacks neatly, Freddie indicated to Matty that they shouldn't speak to Pip while Bumpy was there. So they chatted with Bumpy about the latest news from the front. Matty's father, like Freddie's had also volunteered but he was a sailor, not a soldier, so he asked Bumpy if there was any news from the navy. Just as they finished their tidying, Mrs Greely called out that dinner was ready. All three left the pigeon loft, with Freddie giving a secret wink and smile to Pip as he closed the door, and walked back to the kitchen.

"Matty, you can stay for dinner too," Mrs Greely said and Matty accepted enthusiastically. His mum was working at the munition factory in West Ham, so this was a real treat to have a proper dinner instead of his usual bread and jam sandwich.

Chapter 4
Let's Go Racing

Through the summer Freddie and Matty spent many hours with Pip in the pigeon loft. But Pip and all his friends in the loft were getting restless.

"The thing is," Pip said to Freddie and Matty, "we haven't had any racing since this war started."

"That's a shame," said Matty, "why not?"

"The government has said there's to be no racing while we're at war," Pip said.

"So the only thing we can do, is short flights at dusk for half an hour or so," Pip said with a sorrowful sigh. "We never get out to enjoy these lovely sunny days."

"Why can't they fly during the day?" Matty asked.

"I don't really know," Freddie said, "although when I went shopping with mum the other day, I did hear the butcher say that people were asking for pigeons to put in their pies."

"Pigeon pie!" Pip could hardly contain himself.

"Anyway, that's why Grumpy Bumpy won't let them out. They might get caught."

"I'd like to see them try," said Pip puffing up his chest. "Has he forgotten we're award winning racing pigeons? We're too fast to get caught."

"Hey, I've got an idea," Matty said jumping up and down. "Why don't we take Pip and his friends out and have a race?"

"Hmm," Freddie said, "What if Grumpy Bumpy caught us?"

"Why tell him? This can be a little secret just between us," Matty said, really excited about his idea. And Pip and his friends seemed to pick on the excitement as they all cooed and burbled, ruffling their wings in anticipation.

Freddie looked around the loft and he couldn't help feeling the excitement too. "OK," he said, coming to a decision. "Let's go up to Blackheath and race them there."

Pip looked at Freddie with a shine in his eyes. "Of course, you can't take us in our baskets, your granddad would soon catch us."

'That's true," said Matty, "What are we going to do?"

Freddie put his hand on his chin and thought deeply. Suddenly his eyes lit up, "I've got it, but Pip, you and your friends have to do exactly as I say." Then Freddie whispered his plan to Matty and Pip.

"OK, so we've all got it?" Freddie said.

"Yes sir!" said Pip raising his right wing as if saluting.

"C'mon Matty," said Freddie, and after the two of them had opened all the coops, they went out of the loft and left the door slightly ajar – in fact, just wide enough for a pigeon to hop through. Freddie and Matty then went in search of Grumpy Bumpy, taking with them the newspaper they'd found on the kitchen table. When they found him, they pestered him with questions about almost every article in the paper. After about ten minutes, Freddie gave Matty a secret wink and together they said a cheery goodbye to Grumpy Bumpy, leaving him totally baffled by their odd behaviour.

As they ran up the road towards Blackheath, Freddie puffed out, "Do you think Grumpy Bumpy suspected anything?"

"No, I don't think so," Matty replied. "Oh look, there's the heath."

And just as Freddie and Matty arrived at the edge of the heath they looked up, and flying across the sky came Pip and all his friends. "Gosh, don't they look terrific," said Freddie, feeling a surge of pride that he had set his friends free.

Pip and his friends circled once, then again and then they landed at Freddie's and Matty's feet. "OK, let's start some races," said Freddie, and for the rest of the afternoon Pip, his friends, Freddie and Matty had a marvellous time. Freddie and Matty bet football cards on who would win each race and Pip and his friends circled Blackheath time and time again. But suddenly the fun came to an end.

"'Ere, whaddya kids think you're up to?"

Freddie and Matty spun around as a big shadow loomed over them. Looking up they saw a grizzled face with hard, angry eyes staring at them. Under the nose was an enormous, drooping moustache with little bits of food dangling in it. And on the head was a black, shiny Air Raid Warden's metal helmet.

"Quick, run!" yelled Freddie, and Matty didn't need any more encouragement. Nor did Pip and his friends, who took off in a loud flapping and beating of wings, leaving just a swirl of dust at the feet of the Air Raid Warden. And as the Warden was well into his seventies, he didn't give chase, he just took off his helmet, scratched his head and muttered, "Pesky kids!"

“Phew, that was lucky,” said Freddie as he and Matty walked into Mrs Greely’s kitchen.

“Yeah, I think we got away with it,” Matty replied.

But then both of them stopped. Grumpy Bumpy was standing by the kitchen door with a look as black as thunder on his face. Mrs Greely stood by her cooker with a very sorrowful look on her face.

“So, think you’ve got away with it eh!” growled Grumpy Bumpy. “Think you’ve been clever hey?”

Freddie’s first thought was to pretend ignorance. But then he realised that Matty had given the game away. In fact, he had too by exclaiming they’d been lucky. So his next thought was to smile and see if he could charm his way out of trouble.

“Oh, hello Bumpy, you’re looking very handsome today.”

“Don’t give me that boy,” he shouted. “You waste my time asking lots of silly questions about what’s in the news, while behind my back you let my precious pigeons out!”

Freddie nodded his head slowly, and out of the corner of his eye he saw Matty quietly edging his way out of the kitchen. But Grumpy Bumpy had seen him too.

“STOP!”

Matty froze.

“You were in on it too, so you’re not sneaking off.”

“We’re sorry Bumpy,” Freddie said in a quiet voice.

"Yes, Mr Greely," Matty agreed. "We just thought..."

"Thought," roared Grumpy Bumpy. "Scruffy little boys like you don't think. Mischief, that's all you get up to."

Freddie and Matty stood in the kitchen, their heads hanging in shame. Mrs Greely looked at them kindly, but she knew better than to interrupt granddad. The boys had been naughty and set his pigeons free.

"What if every one of my pigeons has been shot, hey? What are you going to do then, hmmm?" Grumpy Bumpy shouted.

"None of them have been shot Bumpy. I'm sure of it," said Freddie.

"Well let's just go and see hey!" Grumpy Bumpy growled, and he grabbed both boys roughly by their shoulders and pushed them into the garden and towards the pigeon loft.

The loft door was still open, and Freddie felt his heart race in case Pip and his friends hadn't made it home yet. But as he stepped inside the warm, stuffy loft he heard the familiar cooing and rustling of all the pigeons in their coops.

Grumpy Bumpy harrumphed and let go of the boys as he checked each pigeon for any signs of damage.

"You're indeed lucky, they're all here. But don't think this will go unpunished.

As Freddie said goodbye to Matty, they both shook their heads and wondered what sort of punishment Grumpy Bumpy would think of for them.

Chapter 5
Another Lesson is

Freddie was appalled. "No Bumpy, please no. Not that," Freddie pleaded. But it was as if his voice fell on deaf ears. "That's it, my decision is final. You are not allowed in the pigeon loft any more," said Grumpy Bumpy with an evil smile.

"Please, Bumpy, please, please, please," begged Freddie.

Grumpy Bumpy ignored him and picked up the newspaper.

"I'll do anything Bumpy. Sweep, clean, feed and water all the pigeons."

Grumpy Bumpy just rattled his newspaper and turned another page.

"Oh please, please, please Bumpy. I'm sorry I let the pigeons out. I'll never do it again, never, I promise."

"NO!" and Grumpy Bumpy glared at Freddie until he bowed his head and slowly walked out of the kitchen. Standing in the hall, Freddie thought about not being able to see Pip any more, not being able to talk to him... and Pip always had something interesting to say, so it was annoying not being able to talk to him anymore... not being able to feed him or hold him and feel his warm soft body in his hands, or feel Pip's heartbeat thumping away, thump, thump, thump. Lost in his misery, Freddie wondered what he should do, and then he smiled. He'd go and see Matty, he might have some ideas how to win Grumpy Bumpy round.

"Hello Freddie," said Matty as they stood on Matty's front porch. "How's your granddad?"

"Grumpier than ever, and he's banished us from the pigeon loft."

"Oh no," Matty said, shocked. "What will we do, how can we play with Pip now?"

"That's the whole point. Grumpy Bumpy knows how much we love Pip. So I wondered if you had any ideas how we could get him to change his mind," Freddie said hopefully.

"Hmmm," Matty said as he bowed his head in deep thought. "Oh, how about... no, that wouldn't work."

"What?" said Freddie with desperate hope in his voice.

"No, no, it's not worth considering. Now let me see... hmmm. Have you got any money Freddie?"

Freddie frowned as he tried to picture how much might be in his little postbox savings tin. "I think I've got about two shillings, threepence halfpenny," he said at last.

"And what's your granddad's favourite sweetie?" Matty asked next.

"Peppermints," Freddie said, still wondering where this was going, and then it dawned on him.

"Oh good idea Matty! Yes, let's go and buy him a bag of peppermints. He's sure to forgive us then."

About twenty minutes later, after the boys had raided Freddie's savings tin and taken threepence to the sweet shop, they approached Grumpy Bumpy sitting in the sunshine in the garden.

"Don't think you're going anywhere near that pigeon loft you two."

“Oh no Bumpy, we just thought you might like these,” and Freddie handed Grumpy Bumpy a paper bag full of peppermints. Grumpy Bumpy snatched the bag out of Freddie’s hand, looked in, smiled and said, “Thank you lads, I love these,” as he popped one with great delight in his mouth. Freddie and Matty smiled at each other and were just about to wander down to the loft when Grumpy Bumpy yelled at them, “And now be off with you. Go on, go out and play.”

Freddie and Matty smiled sheepishly at Bumpy and turned around and left the garden through the little gate that led onto the lane at the back of the house. “Well that didn’t work did it?” said Freddie.

“No,” Matty agreed and the two of them walked in silence heading for the park.

****

More days went by and Freddie and Matty were still banished from the pigeon loft. They had tried many ways to soften Grumpy Bumpy but he would not relent. More bags of mints had been given and consumed without any change, many cups of tea had been made for and drunk by Bumpy and his shoes had been polished by Freddie daily, but still he said 'NO'.

Eventually, it was Mrs Greely who came to Freddie's and Matty's rescue. The summer holidays were rapidly coming to an end and Freddie was becoming more miserable by the day. Armed with a pouch of Grumpy Bumpy's favourite tobacco that she'd bought only that morning, Mrs Greely approached him and whispered to him that if he gave in and let the boys spend the last few days of summer with the pigeons, she'd also cook his favourite dinner, shepherd's pie followed by a blackberry and apple crumble.

Knowing nothing about the bribe, that afternoon Freddie and Matty were playing soldiers in the garden when suddenly Grumpy Bumpy called to them from the pigeon loft. "Hey boys, come and give me a hand, this sack's too heavy for me to lift on my own."

Kicking over the toy soldiers in their rush to get into the loft before Grumpy Bumpy could change his mind, the boys burst in and immediately started dragging the sack from Bumpy's hands. "Where do you want it Bumpy," Freddie asked.

"Just push it in that corner there, and seeing as you're 'ere now, you might as well give the place a bit of a spring clean," and Bumpy took his pipe and tobacco pouch out of his pocket and shuffled out of the loft. But as he left, he called over his shoulder, "And I hope you've learned your lesson... don't meddle with my pigeons!"

As soon as he'd gone, the boys gave a whoop and went straight to Pip's coop.

"Long time no see," said Pip in a rather droll fashion.

"We're sorry Pip, but Grumpy Bumpy was so angry with us for letting you out, that we were banned from coming to see you."

"Well it's been very dreary here, what with no racing and no news from you," Pip said a little huffily.

But then, seeing how downcast Freddie and Matty looked, he cheered up and said, "Well I think we should join up!"

Freddie and Matty looked shocked. Together they said, "We're too young to join up Pip."

"I didn't mean you two, I meant us pigeons." And Pip puffed his chest up and strutted a couple of steps.

He then told them about how London looked from the air when he was allowed out for a short flight.

Although the German zeppelins were fired on every time they flew over the city, they sometimes managed to drop their bombs and cause terrible devastation.

Freddie and Matty looked at Pip in surprise. Freddie was the first to recover and asked, "How do you know pigeons are allowed to join up Pip?"

"I've met recruits who've been working on the frontlines and with the sea planes."

Matty looked at Freddie and asked, "Is this true... are there pigeons in the army?"

Freddie remembered his granddad reading the newspaper a few months ago, saying the government wanted pigeons. "Yes," he nodded his head, "but Bumpy didn't want to send his pigeons."

At this Pip lifted his head high and gave his wings a shake. “Well if I had an opportunity to serve my country, I would be proud to do it,” and again he strutted smartly up and down in his coop in a rather military fashion. Then a thought occurred to him, “I think you should persuade your granddad to let me go.” But as there was much cooing and fluttering at his remark, he swivelled his head around and looked at all his friends in the loft and said, “In fact, I think your granddad should let us all join up, we all want to do our duty.”

Freddie and Matty looked at all the pigeons cooing and strutting and then they grinned at each other. “I think we’ve got a mission on our hands,” Freddie said to his friend.

“I think you’re right Freddie.”

Chapter 6
A Mission Begins

For the last few days of the summer holidays, Freddie and Matty mounted a campaign to get Grumpy Bumpy to take his pigeons to the recruiting station for pigeons. But each and every time they mentioned it, Grumpy Bumpy would have a sharp reply as to why it was not a good idea. So Freddie and Matty returned to school, and Pip and his pigeon friends were left to fret all day in their loft. But a few days after school had started, on 7 September in the middle of the night, Freddie was woken up by the loudest bang he'd ever heard in his life. The house shook, the pictures on his bedroom wall fell down and it felt like his heart had stopped. He jumped out of bed and ran to his mother's room. He met her on the landing, and granddad was there too, in his pyjamas.

"What is it?" Freddie asked in a trembling voice, "What's happening?"

Mrs Greely pulled Freddie close to her, while Grumpy Bumpy tried to get them down the stairs. "C'mon, down to the kitchen and under the table. It's the safest place to be."

Quickly the three of them scurried down the stairs as more explosions shattered the air and made the house shake again and again. As they sat squashed together under the kitchen table, they heard a deep boom which was repeated and repeated until there were so many booms, they made a frightening rhythm.

"That'll be the anti-aircraft guns. That'll show 'em," said Grumpy Bumpy.

"Show who?" Freddie asked, feeling a bit confused by all the noise and the house shaking.

"The Germans, they're dropping bombs lad."

Mrs Greely saw Freddie's terrified face and pulled him close to her. "Don't worry son, we're alright here," and she frowned at Grumpy Bumpy, willing him to be quiet. The bombing finally stopped in the early hours of the morning, and the anti-aircraft guns fell silent.

By then, Freddie was fast asleep, curled up in his mother's arms. "Seems a shame to wake 'im," Grumpy Bumpy said.

"I know, but we can't stay under this kitchen table all night," Mrs Greely replied and she gently woke Freddie up. Looking all around him at the pots and pans that had fallen to the floor, and the broken crockery that had smashed as it fell from the cupboards, Freddie was shocked. Mrs Greely shook her head at him, , "Don't worry Freddie, you get to bed. This will be alright in the morning."

****

At school the next day, all the talk was about the bombing raid. The east end of London had taken another battering with over 40 bombs being dropped on Woolwich, Deptford, Greenwich, Bermondsey and Rotherhithe.

When school was over, Freddie and Matty ran home to the pigeon loft. As they entered, they saw Grumpy Bumpy picking up and caressing each pigeon in turn. He looked sad and solemn. So the boys backed out quietly and went up to Freddie's bedroom to read his comics. After a while Freddie said, "I wonder why Grumpy Bumpy looks so sad."

“Me too,” said Matty with a puzzled look.

“Shall we go back and see if he’d like some help in the loft?” Freddie asked.

“Good idea,” Matty replied, putting his comic on Freddie’s bed.

But when they entered the loft, there was no sign of Freddie’s granddad. But Pip was there, looking particularly bright eyed and chirpy, and all the other pigeons seemed more animated and noisy than usual.

“It’s happened,” Pip said, and he cooed a bit.

“What’s happened?” Freddie said.

“Your granddad is taking us to the recruitment station,” and Pip seemed to dance on the spot in his excitement.

Freddie and Matty faced each other and smiled. “Hurrah! Pip’s going to be a hero. He’ll help us win the war,” shouted Freddie.

“Oh, just think of it, going over the lines, seeing what the Germans are doing. And then you can fly home and tell us and we’ll tell the army. We’ll all be heroes,” said Matty.

At this, Freddie and Matty did a little dance of their own, thinking about beating the Germans and helping to bring their dads home safely. As they were jumping around, Grumpy Bumpy came into the loft.

“What’s all this noise, and why are you capering around like a couple of mad monkeys? You’ll upset my pigeons”

“Oh, sorry Bumpy, we didn’t mean to do that,” Freddie said.

“Hmmph, well it’s teatime, so you’d better go.”

So Freddie and Matty quietly opened the loft door and left Grumpy Bumpy with his pigeons. "I'd better get home now anyway," said Matty and he gave Freddie a slap on the shoulder and winked at him. Freddie smiled back and whispered, "See you tomorrow hero!"

****

For the rest of the week, Grumpy Bumpy spent most of his time in the loft with his pigeons. If Freddie and Matty came in, he'd find a job for them to do, usually in the garden or running down to the shop on an errand. He hadn't said a word about sending his pigeons to the army, and Freddie was beginning to think maybe Pip had been mistaken. But when Saturday came around, Grumpy Bumpy knocked on Freddie's bedroom door very early in the morning.

"C'mon lad, get up, we've work to do."

This was most unusual, Grumpy Bumpy never made Freddie get up early on the weekend. But Freddie having recently been in Grumpy Bumpy's bad book, got up and dressed and followed his granddad downstairs. Mrs Greely was in the kitchen and she smiled at Freddie. She had made some sandwiches and was wrapping them in brown paper which she then tied up like little parcels with string.

"C'mon Freddie, follow me," said Grumpy Bumpy as he headed out of the door and down towards the pigeon loft.

When he entered, Freddie saw straightaway that all the pigeons' baskets were stacked ready on the floor. He took a deep breath and said, "Are you taking the pigeons somewhere Bumpy?"

"That's right, we are. You and I are takin' them to the recruiting station."

"Really!" Freddie whooped. "All your pigeons are going to be heroes?"

Grumpy Bumpy looked at Freddie with a frown on his face. But as he noticed the joy in Freddie's eyes, he smiled. "That's right boy, heroes each and everyone of 'em. So come on and help me get them in their baskets."

After an hour, Freddie and Grumpy Bumpy had got all the pigeons safely loaded. Bumpy said he was going in for a cuppa, then they'd take the pigeons to the army. Freddie chose to stay in the loft and he went up to Pip's basket. "Well, this is it. You're off to the army Pip."

"And not before time," said Pip. "We pigeons have much to do."

"I'm going to miss you Pip," Freddie said softly.

"Don't you worry. We'll all be back in next to no time," Pip said in his most reassuring voice.

"But there'll be guns, and bombs. I'm frightened," Freddie replied.

"That's exactly why we need to go," said Pip. "The sooner we can beat the Germans, the sooner we can put an end to all this fighting."

Freddie knew in his heart that Pip was right. He knew that's why his dad was fighting. To bring the war to an end. And what Freddie wanted more than anything was to see his dad again. It had been ages since they'd gone hand in hand to see the Gunners play in Woolwich. The best football team in the whole world his dad told him.

"You will be careful, won't you?" Freddie said.

"Of course I will," Pip replied, "we all will."

The door of the loft opened just after Pip said this and Grumpy Bumpy came in. "I've put the trailer out front, so help me load all these baskets on it,"

The trailer belonged to Mr Brown, the greengrocer. He always let Grumpy Bumpy borrow it to take his pigeons out. Of course, before the war, Grumpy Bumpy would take the loaded trailer to the railway station and put his pigeons on a train to where the race would start. This time, he was taking the trailer to the pigeon recruiting station in Woolwich. The wheels were large and the bed of the trailer was level with Freddie's shoulders, so his job was to hand up each basket to his granddad who would then pack them securely. When they had loaded about half the baskets, Matty arrived. "Can I help as well please Mr Greely?"

"Humph, I suppose so. Help Freddie pass the baskets up."

When the trailer was fully loaded, the three of them went into the house to say goodbye to Mrs Greely. Luckily for Matty, she had seen him arrive, so when she handed Freddie and Grumpy Bumpy their parcels of sandwiches, she also had one for him. "Take care as you go," she said, "the roads are still in a terrible state after all that bombing." And she waved them off as Grumpy Bumpy picked up the pulling handle at the front of the trailer and Freddie and Matty pushed from the rear.

Chapter 7
The Mission Takes Off

It was quite a long walk from Charlton to the Woolwich recruitment station, but luckily there was a gentle downhill slope for part of the way. After walking for twenty minutes, they turned on to Repository Road and walked towards the Royal Artillery Barracks. When they got to the main gates, they were met by two sentries who asked their business.

"What does it look like?" Grumpy Bumpy said in a rather angry voice. "We've come to give our pigeons for duty."

"Sorry sir, of course," and the sentry stepped back from the gate. Pointing with his finger, he said, "Take your trailer over there to Shed 14. Corporal Baker will look after you."

Granddad, Freddie and Matty pulled and pushed the trailer towards where the soldier had sent them. The parade ground was enormous and Freddie and Matty were fascinated by all the soldiers who were marching about as if on a mission. There was lots of saluting as soldiers passed officers, and lots of shouting and barking of orders as men were directed from place to place. All this delighted Freddie and Matty, but when Freddie glanced at Grumpy Bumpy, he could see his face was stern and unsmiling.

"This looks like the spot," said Grumpy Bumpy as they came up to a large shed where a couple more trailers stacked with pigeon carrier baskets were waiting by a large open door. A soldier with stripes on his arms and a clipboard in his hands was standing beside a large trestle table and looked as though he was in charge, so Grumpy Bumpy went up to him. "You the boss son?"

The soldier looked up and smiled. "Yes sir, I'm Corporal Henry Baker. I see you've brought some pigeons. The army and country are grateful to you sir."

Grumpy Bumpy looked keenly at the young soldier and harrumphed. Corporal Baker understood this, he realised that a lot of the pigeon fanciers were worried their pigeons would be lost or injured, so he said kindly, "We'll look after them sir. We treat them like the heroes they are." Then he looked at Freddie and Matty who were standing open mouthed staring at all the pigeons already in the shed. They'd never seen so many pigeons together before. Corporal Baker bent towards the boys and said, "And when they're in the forces, the pigeons get the best seed in the world, and plenty of it."

At this, even Grumpy Bumpy smiled as he'd been worried about getting enough seed as his local suppliers were finding it harder and harder to get it in stock.

"Right sir, let's do the paperwork," said Corporal Henry Baker. "You'll receive a certificate from the government listing every pigeon recruited, so can you give me the names and details of your pigeons?"

As Grumpy Bumpy and the corporal did the paperwork, Freddie and Matty helped unload all the baskets and passed them to the soldiers in the shed. But when Freddie took Pip's basket down, he nodded to Matty and they walked away from the trailer. When they were far enough away so that no-one could overhear them, Freddie said, "Pip, we're here, at the recruiting station."

"What's it like?" Pip said.

"Enormous," Freddie replied. "There's a great big shed and it's full of so many racing pigeons, I can't even count them."

"The soldiers are very gentle with all the pigeons too," Matty added, and Freddie smiled at him gratefully. He was worried Pip might regret being sent to war.

"Don't worry boys," said Pip, sensing they were probably more afraid than he was. And then, before any more could be said, a soldier called over to them asking them to bring the basket. As they got back to Grumpy Bumpy, Corporal Baker was handing him a certificate with all his pigeons listed on it. He showed it to them and they read, 'Government Pigeon Service'.

"Gosh," said Freddie, 'it looks very smart doesn't it?"

"And there's something for you too sir," said Corporal Baker, and he picked up a small box from the trestle table and handed it to Grumpy Bumpy. Grumpy Bumpy took it and opened it carefully. Freddie and Matty were studying his face to see if it was good or bad and they were relieved to see a smile spread across his face. Looking at the boys with a wide grin, Grumpy Bumpy showed them what was inside.

"Ooh, that's lovely," said Freddie and Matty together. And they stared with open admiration at the shiny little badge. It was octagon in shape with a bright blue pigeon in the middle and a red crown on top. Around the dark blue edge, written in gold, it said National Pigeon Service. "Pin it on your jacket Bumpy, pin it on your lapel." And with an air of pride, Grumpy Bumpy did just that.

Chapter 8
We're in the Army Now

Pip and his friends had been in the army for a week now and life was very different from being in the loft in Charlton. For a start, there were so many more pigeons on the army base. Pip had expected to stay with all the pigeons from Grumpy Bumpy's loft, but the army had different ideas. They divided the group up and put them into new groups with pigeons from other lofts.

Pip was a little disgruntled at first, but then he decided it was quite exciting to meet all these new characters. His favourites were Bonny Boy from Scotland and Lady Knollys who was almost like royalty as she came from King George V's own loft. Bonny Boy was full of jokes and liked to entertain his new friends with stories about life in Glasgow. One evening he said, "You know, a wee lad came home from school and said to his mam, 'Ach, I got a part in the school play.' 'Awa', ye did' said his mam, 'What part?' 'I'm going to be a Scottish husband,' the wee laddie said. 'You go right back to that school and you tell them you want a speaking part,' said his mam," and Bonny Boy laughed with glee. At first, Pip, Lady Knollys and the other pigeons looked at each other not really understanding the joke, so Bonny Boy said, "Don't you see? Scottish husbands are henpecked. It's the wife gets to call all the shots," and again he laughed.

"Seems very sensible to me," said Lady Knollys. "We ladies are far more intelligent..."

At this point, the rest of Pip's new loft mates set up quite a racket as they debated whether male or female pigeons were the most intelligent. They became so heated on the matter that Private Monty, their handler had to come in and settle them down.

****

"OK recruits," shouted Corporal Henry Baker, "your training at this base will end today."

Corporal Baker was standing in the middle of the loft with Private Monty beside him. "Do you think they understand you?" he asked the Corporal.

"Probably not, but I like to think they can," he said as he gave a cheery wink to the Private. "The new mobile loft is outside, please load all the pigeons in their baskets and then report to me."

"Yes sir!" Private Monty replied as he saluted the Corporal.

"Did you hear that?" Pip whispered to Lady Knollys, who had the coop next to his.

"Yes, I wonder where they're taking us."

"To the front I should think," said Pip, and he gave a little inward shiver at the thought. It wasn't because he was afraid. In fact, he was quite the opposite. He'd been looking forward to doing his duty for King and country, but he knew from meeting other pigeons who had been to the front that it wasn't fun and games out there.

While Pip was reflecting on this, Private Monty put his hands into his coop and gently lifted Pip into a basket that could hold four pigeons. It was soon filled with Bonny Boy, Lady Knollys and another pigeon called Blue Arrow.

The basket was then carried to the mobile loft. If Pip and his friends had been able to see out of their basket, they would have seen they were being loaded onto a London bus that had been converted into their new loft. As soon as all the baskets were onboard, there was a shudder as the engine kicked into life, and then a jolt as the bus rumbled out of the parade ground and off towards Hastings.

It was late afternoon as the mobile loft turned into the Hasting's Army Base.

After several hours of being jolted and shaken over many miles of English country roads, Pip and his friends were glad when they came to a halt. Of course, they had no idea where they were.

Visibility from inside their basket was very limited, and they couldn't see out from the mobile loft at all. As soon as the pigeons realised they were obviously at their destination, they expected to be unloaded and taken to their new coops. But a couple of hours had gone by, and no-one had come in to release them from their baskets.

"Och, I could do with stretching ma wings," said Bonny Boy.

"Me too," said Pip.

"I wouldn't mind a peck of seed," said Lady Knollys.

"And I could do with a drop of water," Blue Arrow chipped in.

But still no-one came. Slowly, the light began to change in the mobile loft as the sun went down. Pip was worried that something terrible had happened and thought that maybe they'd been forgotten. Just as his hope was fading, he heard what sounded like footsteps climbing stairs and then the last light from the sun flooded the loft as the door at the back was opened wide. A familiar voice cheered him as Private Monty called, "I bet you're all hungry hey!"

This was met with a loud cooing as Pip and all his loft mates heartily agreed. But before they were fed, Private Monty and another soldier took each basket out of the loft, and then removed all the pigeons from their baskets and returned them to a coop back in the loft. This took quite a time, but eventually a seed dish and water bowl was given to each pigeon and they could all tuck in.

"Well they weren't too generous with their rations, were they?" remarked Blue Arrow.

"No, I could have eaten that all over again," agreed Pip.

"Ach well, it dinna look like they're giving us more," said Bonny Boy, "I think I'll turn in for the night."

"Me too," said Lady Knollys. And before long, all that could be heard from the loft was the gentle rustling of feathers being settled as sleep descended on each and every pigeon.

Chapter 9
On Our Way

The next day dawned bright and sunny, and everyone in the loft expected to be let out. But instead, all that happened was that the blinds that prevented them seeing out of the loft were removed. Pip blinked and shook his head several times, accustoming his eyes to the daylight.

"Well, I wonder where we are," he said to no-one in particular.

Then he lifted his head and stretched his neck as far as he could. By leaning forward in his coop, he was able to see further. "Oh, I think we're by the coast," he said merrily. "I can see sand dunes."

"Aye, and the air definitely has a salty flavour," agreed Bonny Boy.

"Well, that will mean the Channel is not far away," said Lady Knollys.

"So we're that much closer to France and the front," Pip said with mounting excitement.

Lady Knollys turned her head and fixed her beady orange eye on him. With his chest puffed out, and his head held high, she had to admit to herself he was certainly a very attractive pigeon, and his eagerness for doing his duty only made him all the more appealing. Just as she was considering this, Private Monty clambered up the staircase at the back of the loft and entered. Then, whistling a jolly tune, he filled all the pigeon's water dishes. Pip and all his friends expected to then be let out for a fly around, but they were sorely disappointed.

"Well, this is a rather dreary way to spend the war," said Blue Arrow.

"Yes, I was expecting to be flying around delivering messages," said Pip.

"Perhaps things will get better tomorrow," Lady Knollys suggested. And on that note, all the pigeons settled down for another night of rest.

And the next day certainly did bring a change for everyone. Once again, each pigeon was placed in a travelling basket and packed securely in the mobile loft. As soon as everyone was onboard, the engine rumbled into life and the loft lurched off, making its cumbersome way to Hastings Harbour. When it arrived, Pip and all his friends heard a lot of shouting as people outside seemed to be directing various vehicles and troops to places he could not see.

“Private Monty, have you checked all the baskets are still secure?” asked a deep, rumbling voice that Pip couldn’t identify.

“On my way sir!” Private Monty replied and this was followed by his heavy boots climbing the stairs up to the loft. Once inside, he carefully checked that all the baskets were still safe and secure, and then returned outside.

“All the baskets are tightly secured sir,” he said and the deep, rumbling voice replied, “Excellent, we don’t want to lose our precious cargo to the deep blue sea, do we Private?”

“No sir, most definitely not,” replied Private Monty, and Pip and his friends heard the two soldiers marching off.

“So, we’re at sea,” said Lady Knollys.

“And on our way to the front,” Pip said with a feeling of awe.

Chapter 10
Right in the Thick of It

"Hello Pip," said Lance Corporal Callum, "you've got a special mission today."

Pip raised his head and fixed his bright, shiny eyes on his new handler. It had been three weeks since the mobile loft crossed the English Channel and was driven deep into Picardy, Northern France. During those three weeks, Pip and his friends had been well trained to fly and return to the loft which was called General Head Quarters. And as soon as they returned, there was always a generous helping of seed waiting as their reward. But sometimes the training got a little frightening as soldiers fired guns. The guns weren't aimed at Pip or his friends, but the noise as they were fired was at first very distracting. But all the pigeons soon realised that it was done to help them become accustomed to the sounds of war and before long, they hardly noticed the banging and explosions.

Something else they all had to get used to was having something clipped on each leg. At first it felt strange to Pip to have his identity ring clipped on one leg, and a message carrier on the other, but soon it felt as if this was how it'd always been.

Lance Corporal Callum gently lifted Pip from his coop and put him in a basket which he strapped to his back. This was a new sensation for Pip, he'd never been carried this way before. And then with a great big roar that took him by surprise, he felt as if he was flying through the air although he was still securely held in his basket. This feeling lasted quite some time, but eventually the roaring noise and sensation of flying stopped.

"Here we are Pip," said Lance Corporal Callum as he slowed his despatch motorcycle to a stop. Pip, still in his basket wasn't sure at all where 'here' was but, judging by all the rumbling and thunderous explosions he could hear, he felt pretty sure he was right on the front line. The basket he was in jiggled a bit as Lance Corporal Callum dismounted from his motorcycle, then Pip felt him stride out at a quick pace.

As his boots thumped down some wooden steps, Callum called out, "Anyone home? I've got a gift for some lucky chap." And as he said this, he took Pip's basket off his back. Squinting through the small gaps, Pip realised he was in one of the British Army's trenches. He could also hear quite a lot of voices, some giving orders, and others just swapping cheerful banter.

"I'm looking for one of your pigeon handlers," Lance Corporal Callum shouted above the rumble of noise.

"Oh, that's me," said a chap with a soft Welsh accent. "What have you got there?"

"He's a fine blue and his name is Pip," and Lance Corporal Callum opened the basket and gently removed Pip.

"My, my, you are a good looking bird Pip," said his new handler. "My name is Jack Harley." Pip immediately felt that Jack liked pigeons. His hands were gentle but firm and his voice was friendly in a sing song kind of way.

"Well I'll be on my way," Lance Corporal Callum said. "Pip's a brave bird, he always flew true when training, even with all the guns and grenades going off. Good luck chaps," and off he went with a wave.

"Right Pip," said Jack, "Life is a bit different out here compared to General Headquarters. We're right in the thick of it," and as he said this, he held

Pip in one hand and carried him to a little coop that was tucked into a corner of the trench. As he carefully put him in and filled his water dish he said, "Don't let the noise worry you little man, I'll keep you safe."

Pip was left in his coop for the rest of the afternoon. As there weren't any other pigeons around, it gave him plenty of time to think. He let his head fall onto to his chest and he thought about Lady Knollys, Bonny Boy and Blue Arrow and wondered what they were all doing. Had they been taken from General Headquarters too, or were they still there, waiting for their orders? He felt a little lonely and hoped he'd see them all soon. As night began to fall, Pip thought about Freddie and Grumpy Bumpy, so far away in London. He hoped they were safe and that no more Zeppelins had dropped bombs on them. As he was thinking this, he realised that the constant crashing of artillery had come to a stop and in the silence he let his eyes close and he fell into an uneasy sleep. But it seemed only minutes later that the thunderous roar started again, and he opened his eyes with a start.

The first thing he saw was Jack Harley's friendly face looking at him. 'Good morning Pip, rise and shine as we say in the army," and he opened the coop and took Pip out. He gently wrapped him in a large white cloth, binding Pip's wings so that he couldn't move them. "This is it Pip, we're off over the top. But you'll be safe with me," and Jack carefully tucked Pip inside his uniform jacket. Although it was dark and a bit tight being held so close to Jack, Pip quite liked it. He could feel the warmth of Jack's body and feel his steady heartbeat, which reassured him. Before long Pip could tell they were on the move. It wasn't a smooth journey; sometimes Jack would run along but then he'd crouch down low and scurry forward as if on all fours. Then he'd be up again, running and dashing from side to side, and all the while Pip could hear bullets whizzing by and ferocious shouting, the earth would shudder, the air felt ripped apart by thunderous explosions and sometimes Pip would hear the terrible screams of someone in pain. Yet still, Jack's heart beat stoutly on, and Pip could hear him call to his friends and comrades, cheering them on and keeping them going.

Finally, they came to a stop and an eerie silence fell about them. Inside Jack's jacket Pip was beside himself with curiosity. What had happened? But then a murmur started and slowly Pip could make out words. "Look there... they're falling back."

"Hold your ground lads, let's see what they're up to."

"Sarge, I think they're on the run."

"Harley! Harley, have you got that pigeon?"

Pip was a little disgruntled to hear himself referred to as 'that pigeon' but then realised not everyone knew his name. "Yes, Captain, Pip's here."

"Well get a message off to GHQ. The enemy are turning their flank and they're losing touch with their 21st division. Send a battalion urgently to fill the gap."

Pip could feel Jack writing this down, then he felt himself being taken out of Jack's jacket. The white cloth was removed and a tightly rolled up piece of paper was put in the message carrier on Pip's leg by Jack, and then he lifted Pip up in the air and threw him high. Pip immediately flapped his wings, circled once to get his bearings, and then with a lift of spirits and his own heart beating proudly, he set off for General Headquarters, Picardy.

Chapter 11
Danger in the Air

At first, all went well. It was a clear September day and he could see for miles. But this also meant he was easily spotted from below and he hadn't gone more than a mile before he came under heavy fire. The Germans must be down there he thought, so he quickly repeated the manoeuvres he'd learnt in training. He beat his wings harder than ever and increased his altitude. Before too long the gun fire stopped, those soldiers knew the pigeon was out of reach now. But what Pip didn't know was that they had a trained hawk with them. And just as Pip was relaxing and winging his way back to GHQ, a dark shadow from above fell on him. Quickly looking up Pip spotted what he most feared, a fierce hawk with vicious talons outstretched, ready to capture him.

But as Lance Corporal Callum had said to Jack Harley, Pip and his friends had been trained well. The British soldiers knew that the Germans used hawks to bring their pigeons down, so they had taught the British pigeons a few tricks on how to get away. All Pip had to do was hold his nerve. He had to let the hawk swoop on him at full speed. "Come on, come on," Pip whispered to himself. "Come on, closer, closer."

He looked up again and he could see the razor sharp talons sheering the sky, reaching for him. "Just a little closer," Pip thought, "Just a little more."

Then, as Pip saw the yellow gleam in the hawk's eye, he let himself tumble off his course and fall to the side, and just as quickly righted himself again. But the hawk, not expecting such a clever tactic, didn't have the manoeuvrability to stop his stoop and in a rush of cold air he went racing past Pip, still on his downward journey.

"Well, that was exciting," Pip thought as he rushed on to GHQ.

It was a welcome sight to see his by now familiar GHQ loft. The two signal corpsmen were at their station as Pip came in, circling and getting lower and lower before, at the last minute, he fluttered his wings and landed gently on the loft and into the trapping box. He waited there, but not for long. Private Monty rushed up the loft steps with his usual clatter of heavy boots and took Pip from the box. "Well done boy, well done."

As he removed the message from the carrier, Pip heard him whistle. "I think the Colonel is going to be pleased with this message Pip, and you've delivered it in under fifteen minutes. You must fly like the wind." And with that, Private Monty ran off in a very jaunty manner to deliver the good news to his superior officers.

While Private Monty was delivering the message, his mate Signal Corpsman Noah came up the steps and took Pip from the trapping box. "You've well deserved your feed today Pip," he said, and he took Pip back to his coop and gave him a generous helping of seed.

After he'd eaten his fill, Pip looked around to see who else was in the loft. "Aye, you're back then," Bonny Boy said in his strong Scottish accent. "How did you get on?"

Pip shook his head a couple of times, remembering the fear he'd felt as bullets whistled by and the terror of the hawk's outstretched talons, and then he related his ordeal to Bonny Boy and the other pigeons in the loft.

After this, Pip, Bonny Boy, Lady Knollys, Blue Arrow and all the other pigeons went on many missions with the soldiers in the trenches. Sometimes their loft was moved a few miles too, to keep up with the ever changing front line, but they always managed to find their way back. Life for Pip and his friends continued like this for many months, and their bravery allowed many messages to be delivered from the trenches to GHQ, keeping the lines of communication open when the landlines and telegraph failed.

Then, one bright autumn morning, Private Monty came up to Pip's coop and he took him out. As he was being placed in the now familiar travelling basket, Pip prepared himself for another mission with the soldiers in the trenches. But this time, his journey was longer than usual and when he and the despatch rider eventually arrived at their destination, it was completely unknown terrain to Pip.

"I'll be sorry to see you go," said Lance Corporal Callum, "You've been a good pigeon in our loft, but your courage has earned you a reputation, and now you're moving on to a new home."

Pip put his head on one side as he listened to this and wondered if any of his friends were being moved on too. He looked hard at Lance Corporal Callum with his bright red eye and blinked a couple of times. And, as though he understood Pip's concern, Lance Corporal Callum said in a rather sad voice, "I'm afraid all your friends are staying with us Pip." But realising this tone might upset the brave little pigeon, he
continued, "But I'm sure you'll make lots of new friends here." He then left his motorbike and walked with Pip in his hands towards Pip's new mobile pigeon loft. The signal corpsman on duty looked up as they approached and smiled. "Ah, reinforcements," and he reached out to take Pip from Lance Corporal Callum.

Chapter 12
Metal Monsters

It was September 1916 and Pip had been with his new unit for a couple of weeks. He'd soon got used to the new loft and quickly made friends with the others. They told him many tales of the mud and craters, the explosions and gunfire that was the world these soldiers lived in. Then one day there was great excitement in the camp. A loud, continuous rumbling was heard that at first everyone thought was distant thunder. The pigeons could feel the anticipation of the soldiers as they came in to feed and water them that evening.

"I wonder what all the fuss is about," said one pretty red check pigeon called Ava who had her coop next to Pip's.

"I don't know, but it certainly has everyone on their toes," replied Pip.

The next day the mystery was solved. When the blinds on the loft were opened, Pip and his friends stared out at a line of vehicles unlike anything they'd ever seen before. Likewise, many soldiers were just as baffled by this new arrival. They were enormous grey-green metallic monsters. And unlike cars or motorbikes, they didn't have wheels. Instead they had great big tracks that slowly moved them along.

"What on earth..." began Ava, the pretty red check pigeon. And Pip, who was equally dumfounded, just stared. He had never seen such vehicles before. Suddenly, there was a lot of commotion around the new arrivals as soldiers straightened up and stood at attention. Pip looked to the side and saw a small group of men marching smartly towards the line of grey metallic monsters. They came to an abrupt halt and all the soldiers saluted.

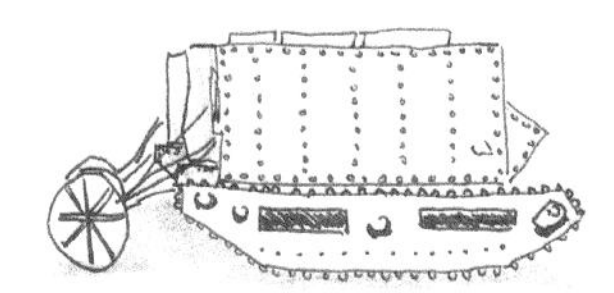

"Right," said Colonel Charles as he faced the soldiers with his legs spread and his hands behind his back. " Meet Little Willie, the Mark 1 tank, our latest weapon against the Huns."

The soldiers remained absolutely silent. Each and everyone of them was worried that they might be asked to drive one of these enormous things, yet many couldn't even drive a car. As if being able to read their minds, the Colonel spoke again. "These armoured vehicles will support you on the field of battle. They can cover terrain that ordinary cars, trucks and lorries can't. They'll cut through barbed wire and they're mounted with guns. "

As he said this, there was a rhythmic thumping that grew louder and louder, and from around a corner of a hut came a platoon of men marching at the double.

"And here are their crew," barked the Colonel.

When the tank crew had come to a smart halt behind the Colonel and Major, the Colonel explained to the rest of the soldiers how the two groups would work together. They would advance towards the Germans, pushing them back and capturing the villages currently under the Germans' control.

In the loft Pip, Ava and the other pigeons were very interested in this new development. "I wonder if we'll be taken in these new tanks," Pip said.

"Oh, I hope not," said Ava. "I like being with my handler, I always feel very safe held close inside his jacket."

But Pip's sense of adventure had been awakened. He liked the feeling when he was carried in a basket on the back of despatch riders, and he now wanted to know what it was like in one of these monster tanks.

****

Pip didn't have long to wait for his new adventure. On a cool, hazy day he was taken from his coop and carried to a soldier standing by a tank. "Here you go mate, this is Pip. Look after him, he's a brave chap who's flown many missions."

The soldier took Pip from the Signal Corpsman and looked him in the eye. Then, with a wink, he expertly wrapped Pip in a large white handkerchief and popped him in a small box which he closed with a snap. "Don't worry pal, I'll make sure he's alright," and he walked away towards his tank.

In his small, dark box Pip couldn't see anything but he felt himself being carried upwards. Then there was a lurch as his box was knocked against something solid. After this, he felt himself swaying slowly to a halt. Recognising the voice of the soldier who had wrapped him in the handkerchief, Pip heard him shout orders to a couple of other men. Then there was an awful shuddering and juddering as the monstrous tank came to life. With a jolt, it moved forward and slowly rumbled its way out of the camp. Pip, in his dark box with his wings held tightly by the handkerchief, swayed and jolted along with the momentum.

The tank moved slowly and with the four men who made up the tank crew packed tightly inside, the temperature soon began to rise. For what seemed like forever to Pip, they swayed and bumped and lurched across rough ground without any relief. The air in the tank was thick with fumes and Pip's head was beginning to feel like it might burst. Because it was so noisy inside the tank from the rumbling of its tracks, it was hard to tell what was going on outside. Suddenly, the man who'd put Pip into the tank shouted, "There they are! That's the Germans in that trench there."

Nothing could have prepared Pip for what happened next. It was the loudest explosion he'd ever heard in his life and it shook every organ within him. But before he could even think about whether he was hurt or not, he was swung violently from side to side as the whole tank rocked backwards and then forwards. Worse still, the crashing explosions and sickening rocking went on and on as the tank crew continued to fire on the Germans. Yet all this was nothing compared to the final explosion. Something burst the wall of the tank and blew up in the confined space where the soldiers were sitting and Pip was strapped. In the deafening aftermath, Pip felt as though his world had come to an end. He couldn't see and he couldn't make sense of anything. Everything had gone silent and black. His instinct was to stretch his wings and fly away, but he couldn't. He was still wrapped tightly and locked in his box.

Pip had no idea how long his world had stopped for, but he realised his box was being opened and he saw a soldier's hand reach in for him. The soldier quickly slipped a message into Pip's carrier and then he threw him through an open flap at the front of the tank.

Pip immediately opened his wings, but to his amazement, instead of flying he tumbled and spiralled to the ground. Again he flapped his wings and tried to take off, but he couldn't. He felt sick and dizzy and his head flopped down. All around him there were explosions, the ground shook and great gobs of earth flew up as shells found their mark. His heart beat rapidly and he was afraid that he would never fly again. But as he lay on the shuddering ground, a picture of Freddie's happy face floated across his mind. He saw him as clearly as if Freddie was right in front of him. And he heard Freddie say, "Pip's going to be a hero," and he realised he couldn't stay where he was. He had to fly, he had to get the message through.

Making a supreme effort, Pip raised himself up and stood shakily for a few minutes. Then he stretched his wings and took off. Up and up he flew. High above all the terrible fighting down below. How silly men are he thought, shooting and bombing each other. Why? What is the purpose of war? And he kept on flying, flying away from it all.

He wasn't sure how long he'd been flying and, for the first time in his life, he wasn't sure where he was or where home was. All he knew was that he had to keep flying, to get away from the killing. And as he flew the day turned slowly to night. He had flown miles across country he didn't recognise. There had been craters and trenches, then woods and a river. He'd seen villages he didn't know and roads he'd never seen before. His muscles were aching, his eyes were tired and he couldn't think clearly any more. He was sad and frightened, worried that he'd let down Freddie, Matty and all the people back home. But his wings just could not beat any longer. He had to rest. Looking down, he saw a small wooded area and he decided that it would be a safe place to spend the night. And with barely realising what he was doing, he landed, tucked his head into his shoulder and went to sleep.

Chapter 13
Something's Cooking

"Je t'ai eu!"

Pip awoke with a start and then his heart started beating violently. Again his wings were pinned as he realised he was in the strong grip of a very heavyset man. He had bushy red hair that stood up all around his head, and in his tiny, sharp eyes there was a look of triumph. Pip nodded a couple of times and then said, "Yes, you most certainly have caught me. Now please let me go."

The man stared at Pip, and then grinned. Pip returned the stare and said in fluent French, "It's true, I'm speaking to you and I wish you to let me go!"

The man laughed harshly and completely ignoring Pip's request, he stuffed him into a canvas satchel he had over his shoulder, and walked off. Pip was too angry to be frightened. His night's rest had completely restored his energy and intelligence and now, all he wanted was to get on his way and fly back to his loft to deliver his message.

The man walked for quite some time, humming happily to himself. After a while, Pip heard the sounds of a working farm. He could hear oxen lowing, and a horse neighing. A few chickens were scratching around and clucking and someone was sweeping.

"Cheri, ma chere," shouted the man, and he started hurrying. The sweeping stopped and a warm voice that Pip presumed was the man's wife, said in French, "What is it Pierre, why are you so excited?"

Jostling Pip in his satchel, the farmer rushed up to his wife and said, "Look, I've found our dinner for tonight!" And he proudly pulled Pip from his bag.

"Oh my, he looks delicious," said his wife as she planted a big wet kiss on the farmer's cheek. And to Pip's alarm, she took him from her husband's grasp and marched into her kitchen.

All day long, Pip waited. He'd been put in a bamboo cage and placed on a counter in the farmhouse kitchen. At least it was warm as there was an enormous fire burning in a big grate on one side of the kitchen, and on the other side there was an old range which the farmer's wife had ominously re-stoked after setting Pip down. As the clock struck four, the family all appeared in the kitchen. As well as the farmer and his wife, there was a young lad who looked about seventeen and a little girl with pigtails. Pip watched and listened. He didn't know why or how, but he understood their French as easily as he understood English. At first the conversation was about the farm and how difficult things were with the occupying Germans taking everything they could and not paying half of what it was worth. As the farmer continued to grumble about how they were being forced into poverty and would hardly have a crust to eat before too long, his wife picked up Pip's cage and said, "Well at least we will eat well tonight."

Pip was terrified. The farmer's wife had big, meaty arms and hands like two great big hams. She grabbed Pip from his cage and laid him down on a chopping board. She then picked up a very large, very sharp knife and held it over Pip's neck.

Pip blinked several times and tried to wriggle free, while calling in his best French, "Stop, stop, please don't kill me, I'm on a mission for the British." But the farmer's wife was oblivious to his calls. Pip wriggled even more as the knife came closer and his little legs kicked up.

Although he didn't intend to hurt the farmer's wife, one of his feet had caught her bare arm and she dropped the knife as the scratch started to bleed.

"Oh, the little brute," she cried out as she held her arm tightly while the farmer himself grabbed both the knife and Pip in his even bigger, stronger hands.

But their little girl had heard Pip and she pulled away her father's hand that was holding the knife.

"Papa, papa, wait!"

Her father raised his shaggy red eyebrows and stared at her. "Ma petite, what do you mean? Are you not hungry?"

"Of course, papa but this little pigeon isn't any ordinary pigeon. He says he works for the British."

Hearing this, her father gave a loud guffaw and started waving the knife perilously close to Pip's neck again. "C'mon papa," said his wife who had now bandaged her arm and had brought a big pot of boiling water to the table, "I want to get this little bird cooked."

"Please, please," Pip yelled, blinking his bright red eye at the little girl. "You must stop them, I have important information to take to the British army."

At this point, the son came nearer to the table and grabbed Pip from his father's grasp and pointing, said, "Hey, look at this, he has something on his legs."

All the family crowded around to get a closer look at Pip's legs. As the head of the family, the father took Pip from his son and studied the ring and the capsule that were fixed to Pip. "Hmmm, this one appears to be some kind of identification," he said, turning the ring with Pip's number on it around in his fingers. "But this one looks like it might hold something, see you can open it."

"Here, give it to me Papa," said his son, "I'll pry it open." Handling Pip gently, he said to his family, "He must be one of the pigeons the British use for intelligence. They send messages in these little containers." Carefully, he held Pip down and took the message container off his leg, then using the nail on his thumb, he pried it open. Inside was the tightly rolled piece of paper that the soldier in the tank had put in.

"What does it say?" asked the little girl excitedly, all thoughts of eating Pip now forgotten.

The son studied the paper hard and wished he'd paid more attention in his English classes at school. But after a while, he said, "Tank hit, out of action. Germans routed, Flers now ours." As one all the family cheered and laughed.

"This is wonderful news," said the father, "the allies are finally pushing the Germans back."

"Well we should reward our little hero," said his wife and she sent her young daughter out to the barn to bring in a handful of seed for Pip. And while they waited, they give Pip a small clay dish of water. At once Pip drank it up; he was very thirsty as he hadn't eaten or drunk anything for a long time. As he ate the seed, the family discussed what they should do with him.

Chapter 14
Set Free At Last

"We must be very careful," said the father. "I've seen the notices that the Germans have put up. People can be shot if they don't hand the pigeons in." His little girl started to shake and even her pigtails began trembling when she heard this. "Don't worry ma petite, they won't know."

"They better not," said his son, scaring his younger sister even more. "They fine the whole village thousands of francs as well."

"So what are we going to do?" asked the farmer's wife.

Pip said. "Send me home, send me home. Put my message back and send me home." And before the little girl could repeat this, the son said, "Let's put his message back and release him. Maybe he'll find his way back home."

Pip thought, if only I had arms, I might hug him. But then the father said, "That's all very well, but I think we can do better than that." His son looked at him and waited. "I happen to know someone in the resistance who would probably like to send more information to our friends the allies." This time his whole family looked at him in quiet amazement. "Say nothing more,' said their father as he tapped his nose. "Too much information is dangerous for you. Here, give me the pigeon."

He slipped the original message back into Pip's carrier on his leg, then wrapped a cloth around him and popped him back in his canvas satchel and walked out the door. As he left, he turned and said, "I won't be long, have dinner ready when I return." When he heard these words, Pip heaved a sigh of relief. He was no longer destined for the pot.

About twenty minutes later the farmer, with Pip swinging in the satchel over his shoulder, knocked on a door. There was a whispered conversation which included a lot of nonsense questions and answers that Pip could only assume was some sort of secret code, and the door was opened. The farmer hurried through and the door was quickly shut and locked again.

"You took a big risk Pierre," said a soft, lilting voice that obviously belonged to a lady. This surprised Pip, he didn't know that ladies were involved in intelligence in the war.

"But it's important. This is a British pigeon and he's got a message concerning Flers. The allies overcame the Germans and pushed them back."

"That's wonderful news," said the lady in her soft, gentle voice.

"Yes, and I thought it might be an opportunity for you to send some additional intelligence."

After a thirty seconds of silence, a light cheerful laugh came from the stranger. "You are a smart man, Pierre. Here, give me the pigeon. You had better hurry home. You don't want to be caught by any rogue patrols."

"You're right, au revoir," said the farmer and Pip heard him leave.

Pip waited at attention on an old desk in the study of this new French woman as she penned a message on a sheet of paper. As soon as the ink was dry, the message was put in Pip's message carrier and he was carried outside and set free.

Pip flew up in ever ascending circles, getting his bearings. His day of rest after being released from the tank had cleared his head, and the seed and water had renewed his strength and energy. It didn't take him long to find magnetic north, and he was soon flying at his maximum speed of twenty miles an hour. Within in hour he saw his latest pigeon loft and slowed down for his approach and landing. The two signal corpsmen on duty pointed to him and one immediately ran up to the trapping box. Before too long, the Colonel had Pip's message and relayed it to GHQ. When GHQ heard that Pip had been used to collect intelligence from behind enemy lines, a request was sent for Pip's rapid return and the next day, he was back his old loft.

After his first unexpected foray into intelligence gathering, Pip was constantly on call for intelligence duties. He was often taken up in spotter planes and released with messages telling where the German gun nests were. He liked these missions as he was flying without actually flying until he was released.

He was also taken out in tanks again, and although he didn't like these missions so much, he knew what to expect and he found if he stayed calm and breathed slowly, he could cope with the giddiness caused by the awful fumes.

But his last few missions were always behind enemy lines. He was taken up in an aeroplane and then dropped out in a little box that had a parachute attached to it. He carried messages for the French resistance to find, asking them to send information on German morale and any other intelligence they could pick up in bars and cafés.

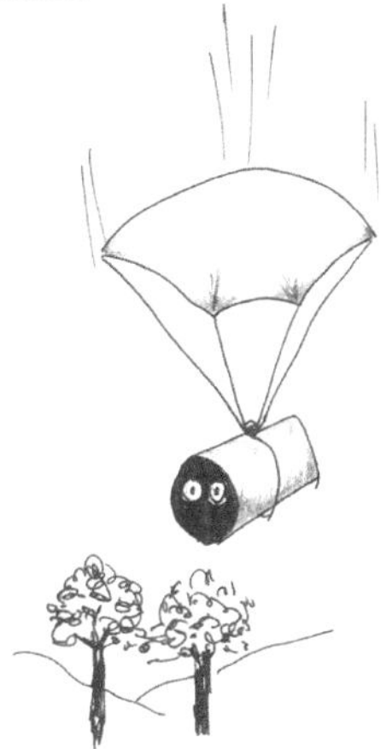

Pip was lucky and was never found by any Germans or their spies. Instead he was able to deliver vital information to headquarters. One of the major turning points for the British and their allies was information Pip brought back about Germany's plans for a big showdown at Marne-Rheims. In his little message carrier there were details on troop movements, their numbers, locations, the lack of supplies the Germans had and, most importantly, their loss of hope for winning the war. Knowing all this and knowing how tired the German troops were, the British and the allies planned a counter attack which led to a great victory for them.

Finally, after four long years of fighting, the Germans realised they were beaten. With Pip and his many friends flying across the battlefields, delivering vital information, all the countries who had joined forces against the Germans pushed the battle weary Germans back with victory after victory. Realising they had no alternative, the Germans gave up and signed the treaty admitting their defeat on 11 November 1918.

Chapter 15
A Happy Reunion

It was a Saturday morning and Freddie was in the garden helping Grumpy Bumpy tidy up. During the night a strong wind had blown his sprouts down, so the two of them were banging wooden stakes into the ground to give the plants some support.

"Brrr, it's cold out here," said Freddie as he held another stake steady for Bumpy to thump.

"You're not working 'ard enough lad. C'mon, you have a go at whacking the stakes in. That'll warm yer." And he handed Freddie his lump hammer. At first, Freddie could hardly swing it, so Grump Bumpy took it back and showed him how to hold it firmly with two hands and then swing it in a circle, landing on top of the stake. After a few swings, Freddie was soon in his stride and he felt a warm glow spreading through him. "Just mind you miss my fingers," Bumpy said.

Suddenly they heard a light scream and then shouting coming from the kitchen. Alarmed, they dropped the stakes and hammer and ran in, worried something awful had happened. Instead, they too started shouting and laughing because Mr Greely, Freddie's dad stood there in his army uniform, hugging Mrs Greely tightly.

"Well, that's a turn up for the books," said Grumpy Bumpy, and he gave his son a hearty slap on the back.

Freddie was delighted. He skipped about and fired a thousand questions at his dad, who had no time to answer before another hundred were asked.

Finally, their commotion died down and they all stood smiling and hugging one another until Mrs Greely said "Get the kettle on Bumpy, and you get the cups and saucers out Freddie. I bet you can't wait to have a good cup of tea can you?" and she lightly kissed her husband on the cheek.

Later that night, when he was in bed, Freddie kept smiling to himself. He was so glad his dad was back home, safe and sound. He hadn't said much about what he'd been through, but Freddie didn't mind, he was just pleased to have him back. And then his thoughts turned to Pip. Ever since they'd dropped him off with Grumpy Bumpy's other pigeons, they hadn't heard a thing. Whenever Freddie asked, Bumpy said it was army business and not for the likes of them to know what was going on. But now, with dad back, Freddie was sure Pip would come home too, and he drifted off to sleep with that thought in mind.

As it turned out, Pip did shortly follow Mr Greely home. And so did all the others from the loft. Grumpy Bumpy simply beamed when he got the notice to pick his pigeons up from the barracks. So off he went on a Saturday morning with Freddie, Mr Greely and Matty. All the way there, as they pushed Mr Brown's trailer, Freddie and Matty discussed whether Pip would be injured, would he remember them, would he still be able to speak to them.

They weren't disappointed. As soon as they saw Pip they could see he was all in one piece and as handsome as ever. And as they loaded his basket onto the trailer, Pip whispered a quick hello.

That night, when all the pigeons were back in their familiar loft, there was so much cooing between them that Freddie couldn't get a word in edgewise. He looked at Pip with disappointment, but Pip reassured him that tomorrow he would be back to his usual self and would talk all day with him, but tonight it was a pigeon reunion. Freddie nodded and said he understood, but he felt a little bit left out. Then he remembered his dad had promised to play cards with him until bedtime, so he skipped off quite happily.

The next day, Freddie got up before the rest of the family and let himself into the pigeon loft. He went around all the coops, giving each bird a little seed and water, and then he settled down on a sack of seed and listened to all